Raging Waters

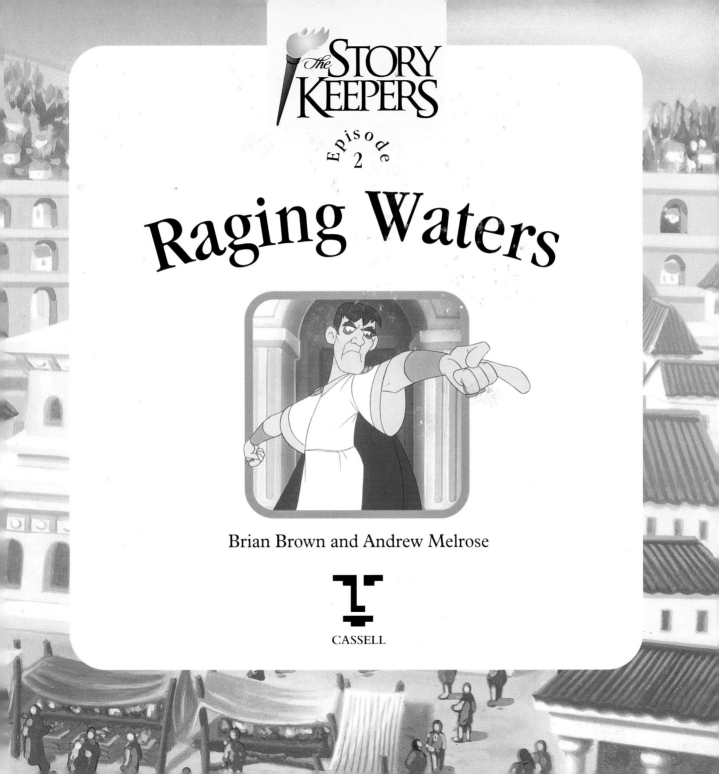

THE STORY KEEPERS

Episode 2

Raging Waters

Brian Brown and Andrew Melrose

CASSELL

Cassell
Wellington House, 125 Strand,
London WC2R 0BB

First published 1996

**British Library Cataloguing-
in-Publication Data**
A catalogue record for this
book is available from the
British Library.

ISBN 0-304-34689-6

Long ago, in the city of Rome,
there lived a mighty ruler.
His name was Nero.
He thought he was a god,
but the Christians knew he wasn't.
So Nero hated them.

One day there was a great fire.
Nero said the Christians started it,
and he sent his cruel soldiers after them.

Marcus, Justin, and Anna
lost their parents during the fire.
Ben the baker and his wife, Helena,
took them into their home.
There, in a time of great danger,
they told the children stories about Jesus.

This book is about the adventures
of the Storykeepers.

"Look at this!" Ben called.
He tossed a piece of dough
and balanced it on his nose.
Justin, Anna, and Cyrus laughed.
But Helena was worried.
"Where is Zak?" she asked.
"I hope he is all right."

But Zak wasn't all right.
Soldiers were chasing him,
and he was running for his life.
He ran down the street.
He climbed over walls.
But they cornered him.

Quickly he jumped
onto a horse.
The horse threw him
over a wall into a
fountain.
He ducked under the
water so the soldiers
could not see him.

When the soldiers went away, Zak ran back to the bakery.
"Bad news!" he told Ben and Helena.
"The storykeeper in North Rome was captured!
Who will tell a story to the Christians there tonight?"
"I can't go," said Ben.
"I am telling a story here tonight
about a man called John."

John lived in the desert.
"Someone very important
is coming," he told the people,
"so stop being selfish. Share what you have."
Many of the people wanted to change their ways.
So he baptized them in the river.

Not long after,
Jesus arrived at the river bank.
Just like the others,
Jesus asked John to baptize him.

Then something wonderful happened.
Jesus came up out of the water.
He looked up.
The clouds above him opened.
He heard a voice:
"You are my only Son.
I am pleased with you."

"That's a great story," said Zak,
"but what about the Christians
in North Rome?"
"I have another story for them,"
Ben replied.
He wrote the story on a scroll
and hid it in a loaf of bread.
"Take this to them, Zak,"
he said.

"What about the soldiers?" asked Zak.
"We know a way," said Anna.
"We could use the water channels."
"Good idea!" said Zak.

Zak, Anna, and Cyrus used a barrel
to float along the water channels.
They laughed and splashed each other.
Suddenly the barrel tipped.
They fell in the water and landed in
a filter station.

Roman soldiers pulled them from the water.
"What's this?" Stouticus said.
He grabbed the bread from Zak and took a bite
– right into the scroll!
Tacticus grabbed the scroll.

"A Christian!" he said to Zak.
"You're under arrest."
Anna ran back to the bakery.
"They captured Zak!" she cried.
"And Justin and Cyrus
followed them."
"What can we do?" said Ben.
Helena had an idea.
"Let's bake some special cakes
for Nero," she said.

Still following Zak, Justin and Cyrus
sailed right under Nero's palace.
They climbed through a grating
and hid behind a statue
in Nero's throne room.

They could see everything.
Nero was singing.
Tacticus dragged Zak in front of Nero.
"We captured this Christian in the waterway,"
he told Nero.

"What is he holding?"
demanded Nero.
"Some kind of story
about this Jesus,"
Tacticus replied.
"Read it, Christian,"
ordered Nero.

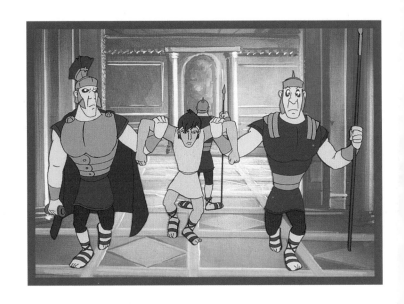

"No," replied Zak, "you only
want to make fun of Jesus.
I'd rather die than read it."

"Very well,"
Nero snapped.
"Soldier, you read it."
"Jesus and his disciples
were in a boat on a lake,"
Tacticus began.

20

Jesus was asleep in the stern.
Suddenly a terrible storm came up.
The waves poured over the side of the boat.
The disciples were terrified.

"Master, please wake up!" they shouted at Jesus. "Don't you care if we drown?" "Silence! Be still!" Jesus ordered. As he spoke, the wind and the waves died down. The sea was calm again.

"What kind of man is he?" the disciples asked. "Even the wind and the sea obey him."

"What a stupid story!" exclaimed Nero. "Throw this boy to the lions."

Justin and Cyrus saw it all. "I hope Ben gets here soon," Justin whispered.

Four strange figures came to the palace.

They were dressed as bakers from Gaul.

They pretended to speak like French people.

"We have brought a cake for the emperor," they said.

"And a poison cake for the prisoner."

Nero was delighted.
He handed the cake to Zak.
Zak realized who the baker
was. So he bit the cake.
He fell to the floor and
pretended he was dead.

Ben and Helena put Zak on the cart.
They started to take him away.
Then Zak sneezed.
Nero was furious.
"Stop them!" he ordered.
They were trapped.
"Ben! Over here!" whispered Justin.
Justin and Cyrus pushed over the statue.
Crash! It fell on the cart.
Flour filled the room.

Ben and the gang jumped through
    the grating under the statue.
        Tacticus gave Zak the scroll.
 "Hurry, before I change my mind,"
he said.
Zak jumped and landed
on Justin's barrel.
"After them!" shouted Nero.

The soldiers chased them.
Ben and the children held on tight.
They escaped through the water.

Ben threw the scroll.
Some friends below
caught it.

That night, thanks to
Ben and the children, the
Christians in North Rome
had their story after all.

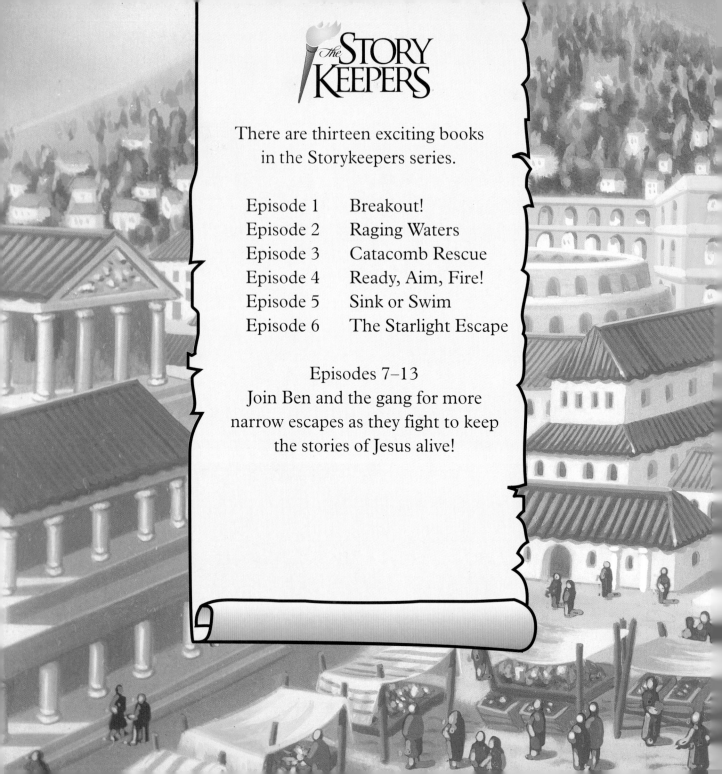

THE STORY KEEPERS

There are thirteen exciting books
in the Storykeepers series.

Episodes 7–13
Join Ben and the gang for more
narrow escapes as they fight to keep
the stories of Jesus alive!